TROLL HUNTERS

Raintree

www.raintreepublishers.co.uk
Visit our website to find out
more information about
Raintree books.

To order:
☎ Phone 0845 6044371
🖷 Fax +44 (0) 1865 312263
🖳 Email myorders@raintreepublishers.co.uk

Customers from outside the UK please telephone +44 1865 312262

Raintree is an imprint of Capstone Global Library Limited, a company incorporated in
England and Wales having its registered office at 7 Pilgrim Street, London EC4V 6LB
Registered company number: 6695882

Text © Stone Arch Books 2012
First published by Stone Arch Books in 2012
First published in the United Kingdom by Capstone Global Library in 2013
The moral rights of the proprietor have been asserted.

Editor: John-Paul Wilkins
Designer: Hilary Wacholz
Printed and bound in China by Leo Paper Products Ltd

ISBN 978 1 406 24726 8 (paperback)
16 15 14 13 12
10 9 8 7 6 5 4 3 2 1

.British Library Cataloguing in Publication Data
A full catalogue record for this book is available from the British Library.

Skyfall

BOOK 1

WRITTEN BY MICHAEL DAHL

ILLUSTRATED BY BEN KOVAR

CONTENTS

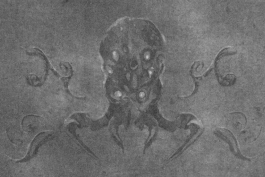

To H.P. LOVECRAFT,
SPELEOLOGIST

Beneath the roots of tree and vine,
Beneath the grimmest grave,
Beneath the deepest, darkest mine,
Beneath the dimmest cave,

Beneath the vast volcanic lakes,
Beneath the fiery core,
An ancient, ageless Evil wakes
And starts to rise once more.

— from *The Pit of Trolls* by Orson Drood.

ONE NIGHT…

Pablo O'Ryan didn't believe in monsters.
He didn't believe in vampires, werewolves,
trolls under bridges, giants, or ghosts,
either. He was too old for that kind of stuff.
But by the end of the night – the night the
stars fell on Zion Falls – not only would he
believe in monsters . . .

…HE WOULD HAVE TO FIGHT THEM.

1

THE BIG BAD WOLF

County Road One ran east out of Zion Falls, snaked around the north edge of the old, abandoned quarry, and then stretched east again in a straight line. It ran past empty fields, pathless woods, and a few old, weather-beaten houses. Some homes still had people living inside them. A mile from the quarry stood the shack where Lionel Tooker lived with his little girl, Louise.

Lionel Tooker had a red beard, long hair, several hunting rifles, and no patience for other people. Seven-year-old Louise was the same.

Louise preferred to spend time with her rabbits, rather than with her schoolmates. But one morning, Mr Tooker and his daughter awoke to find that the top half of the wire screen on the rabbit cage in the back garden had been ripped off. Several of the rabbits were missing.

Their back garden bordered on a dark, thick section of woods. Mr Tooker set up a metal leghold trap in the woods not far from the rabbit cage.

"Don't worry, Louise," he told the sobbing girl. "We'll catch that big bad wolf. He won't take any more of your bunnies, okay?"

Mr Tooker didn't really believe it was a wolf that had snatched the furry pets. He was sure it was something smaller, like a coyote or a fox.

Mr Tooker was also sure that the trap would take care of it.

That night, the night the stars fell, Mr Tooker grabbed a shotgun and a torch. He wanted to see if his trap had caught anything.

"Stay right there, Louise," he warned. Then he headed into the woods. The little girl, wearing just her nightdress, stood next to the rabbit cage. She held one of her remaining pets in her arms. Its soft ears tickled her chin.

Mr Tooker stepped deeper into the shadow of the trees. After a few more steps, he disappeared into the darkness.

A moment later, he let out a shout.

"It's gone!" Mr Tooker yelled.

The trap had been chained to the thick trunk of an elm tree. The chain, the trap, and half the tree's branches were missing.

"I don't get it," Mr Tooker said. "What could have done this?"

Something heavy crashed through the bushes behind him.

Mr Tooker turned around and screamed. Louise dropped her rabbit. It scooted away through the grass and into the darkness. The little girl opened her mouth to yell, but nothing came out. She ran back to the shack and crawled under her bed.

"The big bad wolf," Louise said. "The big bad wolf."

2

Impact

Less than a mile away from the Tookers' shack, an argument was heating up in the back garden of the O'Ryan home.

"We're not going anywhere tonight," Mr O'Ryan told his fourteen-year-old son.

"But we have to go and see the Draconids," Pablo said. "It's the biggest meteor storm of the century!"

"Draconids?" asked his father. "What are Draconids?"

"The meteors come from the direction of the constellation Draco," Pablo explained.

"We can see them just fine from the back garden," argued his father.

"But the quarry is the best place to watch the shower," said Pablo.

"Why?" his father asked. "The sky looks exactly the same from here."

Pablo's mother was unfolding a plastic garden chair. "There's that big lake at the bottom of the quarry," she said. "You could see the meteors from above and from below at the same time."

"Like a giant mirror," Pablo added, nodding.

Pablo gazed up at the starry sky. His friends, Thora and Bryce, were going to the quarry, but he knew that wouldn't make any difference to his father. He was a stubborn man. He was also shy, and he hated crowds.

"The sky is big enough to see from right here," Pablo's dad said quietly.

Pablo stormed into the house and then up the stairs to his bedroom. A few moments later, his mother appeared outside his door.

"I just don't understand," said Pablo. "Why can't we go to the quarry?"

Mrs O'Ryan folded her hands. "I've already set up the lawn chairs," she said. "And I brought out the binoculars for you."

"I'm not going to watch," said Pablo. He kicked off his shoes and sat down on his bed.

His mother sighed. "I'd hate for you to miss it," she said. She started to leave, but then turned back to face Pablo. "We'll be outside if you change your mind."

Pablo waited until he heard his mother go through the kitchen and out of the back door. Then he locked his door. He had promised Thora that he would meet her and Bryce at the quarry. He was going to keep his word.

Pablo walked to his open window, slipped on to the sill, and eased his way down to the ledge beneath. Then he stretched out his legs, released his grip, and landed on the soft grass in his bare feet.

He stood still, listening. His parents were talking in the back garden. Pablo silently headed down the long, winding driveway. A moment later, he was walking along County Road One. The tarmac felt warm on the soles of his feet as he headed west.

The road was dark. There were no streetlights that far out from town.

Pablo pressed the light on his watch to check the time. He still had a few minutes before the first meteors would slice through the atmosphere.

Pablo glanced at the deep, grassy ditches that ran along both sides of the road. Beyond the ditches were endless walls of trees, black against the starry sky.

I must be close to the abandoned Nye farm, he thought.

The creepy old Nye twins had that deep well on their land. The well that grown-ups had always warned Pablo and his friends about when they were kids. "If you fall in," Pablo's dad had said, "no one will ever find you."

Pablo's thoughts were interrupted by a car rumbling up from behind.

Pablo turned just in time to be blinded by a pair of headlights. He quickly stepped aside as a huge off-road vehicle quickly whooshed past. *They didn't even slow down*, he thought.

The car was heading west towards the quarry. Pablo recognized the car. It belonged to the Fishers.

Zak Fisher was in the same year as Pablo, but they didn't hang around with the same people. Zak was one of the popular kids, muscular and talkative. Pablo was the quiet type. He did his homework, kept his head down, and tried his hardest to avoid the school bullies.

Suddenly, the scream of braking tyres split the night air. The car stopped abruptly, as if it had collided with an invisible wall.

The rear window shattered as the bonnet of the car flew upwards. Pablo heard a long, low growl accompanying the cries of human voices. It made him think of a large animal in pain.

Then, just beyond the wreck, Pablo saw what looked like two eyes blink shut. *Did I just imagine that?* he thought.

Pablo found himself running towards the car. He saw three or four figures inside. One of the passenger doors opened and Zak Fisher staggered out. Blood ran from his nose and forehead.

"O'Ryan," he said. "What are you doing here?"

"Are you all right?" asked Pablo.

Zak looked at Pablo blankly for a moment. Then he bent over and threw up in the middle of the road.

Zak stood up, patting his sweatshirt and jeans. "I . . . I have a phone," he mumbled. As he pulled the mobile phone out of his pocket, the crushed device broke into several pieces. "Oh, no . . ."

Pablo thought angrily about his father again. *If my dad would have let me have a mobile phone*, he thought, *then I could call 999 right now.*

"Forget it," said Pablo. "I'll run home and get help."

"I'll come with you," said Zak.

"You should stay with your family," said Pablo. But Zak just ran past Pablo, heading down the road. Pablo ran after him.

In minutes, both boys were running up the dirt driveway to the O'Ryan house.

Pablo couldn't shake the feeling that something was very wrong. The Fishers' car had been wrecked, but there was no sign of what it had hit.

Whatever it was, Pablo thought, *it must have been big.*

3

THE FOURTH STAR

Thora Gamble stared at the dark, calm lake water while her older brother, Bryce, stared up at the stars. "Hey – did you see that one?" cried Bryce. He shook Thora's shoulder and pointed skyward.

"Yes," she replied. "I see it."

Her brother held his phone at arm's length and snapped a photo. "That's so cool."

In the few minutes since the Draconid shower began, Thora had already seen dozens of the shooting stars.

Thora preferred watching the meteors in the giant reflecting pool of the quarry's lake. Seeing the stars far below her feet and overhead at the same time gave her a woozy, floating feeling.

I feel like I'm flying through the air, Thora thought, smiling. *Flying like a dragon.*

Staring down at the lake also made Thora feel very alone, as if the crowds of people who surrounded her weren't even there. Just her and the stars above . . .

She barely noticed the oohs and aahs the crowd breathed whenever an especially bright star skimmed across the sky. For some reason, the arrival of the Draconid shower seemed like a wonderful, personal gift that was just for her.

Thora's birthday was only a few days away, so the timing of this spectacular, once-in-a-lifetime event couldn't have been more perfect. Her mind seemed to soar across the stars.

"Oooh, look," Bryce said, snapping Thora back to Earth. "That one's racing right past Orion's belt!"

Thora nodded. She gazed down at the shining meteor that flashed across the watery mirror. Orion was one of the easier constellations to find – Thora could spot Orion's famous belt by the four bright stars in a row.

Wait – four? Thora thought, puzzled. *There's only supposed to be three.*

Thora blinked and looked again at the starry belt reflected in the quarry's lake.

Then Thora counted the stars one more time just to make sure. *Four stars, no doubt about it,* she thought. *Weird.*

Thora quickly glanced back up at the sky. There was the real Orion, blazing overhead, just as he had for centuries, the legendary hunter who had conquered monsters and giant scorpions. Thora gazed at his belt. *One, two, three,* she counted in her head. *Only three stars. That's right.*

But when she looked down into the lake again, four stars glimmered on Orion's belt.

Thora gasped. The fourth star was moving slowly towards the edge of the lake.

4

BLOOD AND STARLIGHT

Pablo was breathing hard as he ran towards his house. But just as he reached the door, he heard his mother scream. When he rushed inside, he saw that Zak had collapsed on to a kitchen chair. More blood stained his hooded sweatshirt.

Pablo's mother grabbed a flannel from the sink and began gently wiping Zak's face.

"What's wrong?" said Pablo's father, rushing in.

"What happened to you, Zak?" asked Mrs O'Ryan.

Zak didn't respond. He just stared ahead blankly.

"Stella, the boy's in shock," said Mr O'Ryan. He turned towards his son. "Pablo, what the heck is going on?"

Pablo was still gasping from the run. He took a few deep breaths. "It was an accident," he said. "The Fishers. Their car. Out on the road."

Mr O'Ryan glared at his son. "What were you doing out on the road?" he asked.

"Zak's parents," Pablo explained to his dad. "They were hurt in a car accident."

Zak suddenly bolted to his feet. "I have to go," he said dazedly. "I have to help them."

"Both you boys should stay right here," said Mrs O'Ryan.

"I'll go," said her husband. He grabbed a torch from a kitchen drawer and pulled his jacket off the hook next to the back door.

"Please, please," said Zak, standing up. "I have to go!"

Mr O'Ryan braced the boy's shoulders and gently sat him back down. "You're not going anywhere," he said. "Stella, call 999. I'll go and see if Zak's parents are all right."

Mr O'Ryan disappeared out of the back door as Pablo's mother snatched at the phone and tapped in the emergency numbers.

Zak touched his nose with the sleeve of his sweatshirt and then looked at it. Blood had dripped on to the fabric. "It's not so bad," Zak said.

"You're missing a shoe," said Pablo.

"Yeah?" Zak looked down. "Well, you're missing both of them." A confused look spread across his dark features. "Were you in the car, too?" he asked.

"You're in shock, Zak," said Pablo.

Zak stared at Pablo. "Please help me."

Pablo felt compelled to look into Zak's eyes. A strange light flickered there. It was something Pablo had never noticed before. It was almost as if a light shone from within them. *Like starlight,* Pablo thought.

It reminded Pablo of the wild eyes he had seen blinking beyond the crushed car bonnet. Or had he only imagined them in the horrible rush of events?

"Please, Pablo," said Zak. His eyes sparkled.

Pablo nodded.

"Then come on." Zak dashed towards the kitchen door.

Both boys raced outside. "Pablo!" yelled his mother. But both boys kept running, heading down the driveway to the road.

Pablo's thoughts were racing. *I hope he doesn't pass out while he's running. Is his blood dripping on to the grass? Am I stepping in it? Yuck! I'd better watch out for broken glass on the road . . .*

It took them only a few moments to reach the wreck. Smoke rose from the car's hood. Mr O'Ryan was yanking on the driver's door handle. He turned to face the boys as they approached.

"What happened here?" asked Mr O'Ryan.

"Something ran out on to the road," said Zak, stepping closer. "And that's when –"

The door finally opened with a screech. Pablo's father's eyes went wide.

Oh, no. Pablo thought. *Are the Fishers dead?* He raced up beside his father and stared into the car.

It was empty.

5

FLEEING THE WOLF

At the lake, Thora scrunched up her nose. "What's that smell?" she asked.

Several children began coughing. The grown-ups standing near the edge of the quarry covered their noses. A few dogs barked and whined.

"Don't look at me," Bryce said, laughing. "She who smelt it, dealt it." But even he was covering his face.

The smell reminded Thora of rotten eggs, old cat litter, and cigarette smoke. She couldn't tell where it was coming from.

The lake, maybe? She gazed carefully at the water, but the extra star was gone now.

"I can't take this smell anymore," said Bryce. "Let's go."

Thora and Bryce gathered their things and threw them into his car. Other stargazers were returning to their cars, too. Car engines revved up around the quarry as people waved farewell to their friends and neighbours. But closed doors and windows were no barrier to the overpowering smell.

Bryce and Thora were the only ones heading east. While most of the people drove west to Zion Falls, the Gambles lived further east off County Road One.

Thora sniffed. The awful scent was still hanging in the air. "Think it's dangerous?"

Her brother laughed. "It's probably just sulphur or something like that from the lake." Then he added, "Whatever it is, it stinks – and it stinks that we had to leave early. Pablo wasn't even there yet."

Thora had once read how people in ancient times sometimes saw glowing gas fumes hovering over swamps. The glow had been mistaken for ghosts. *Maybe the fourth star on the lake was just natural gas escaping from the quarry lake*, thought Thora.

"What's that?" asked Bryce.

Thora looked up. Her brother was gripping the steering wheel so tightly his knuckles were pale. At the far end of the road was an orange glow. A pale finger of flame flickered behind some trees.

"It's a fire!" said Bryce.

"I hope it's not the O'Ryans' house," said Thora.

"Me too," said Bryce.

Thora's heart pounded. Pablo had promised that he would watch the meteor shower with them at the quarry . . . and Pablo never broke a promise.

"Don't worry," said Bryce.

Thora kept gazing at the weird glow. "Maybe it's a forest fire," she said.

Suddenly, a small white figure appeared in the middle of the road. "Look out!" Thora screamed.

Bryce shouted and slammed his foot on the brake pedal. The car stopped a few feet away from the figure.

"It's a kid," said Bryce.

"It's Louise Tooker!" said Thora. She jumped out of the car and ran over to the little girl.

Louise, still wearing her nightdress, was screaming and crying. Tears streamed down her face.

"What's wrong?" asked Thora, kneeling down. "Are you okay?"

The little girl ran into Thora's arms and sobbed.

"There, there, it's all right," said Thora.

"What's wrong?" asked Bryce. "Is it your house? Is your house on fire?"

The girl continued to sob and gasp. Bryce tapped 999 into his phone.

"What is it, Louise?" asked Thora.

Louise gazed up at Thora with fearful eyes. "Big b-b-bad . . ." she stuttered.

Just then, another, larger shape stepped out of the grassy ditch alongside the road. Thora held her breath. It was a man with a red beard, a pale face, and haunted eyes.

"Mr Tooker!" yelled Bryce.

"That . . . that *thing* burned down my house," said Lionel Tooker.

Louise buried her head in Thora's shoulder. "The big bad wolf," she cried.

Bryce snapped his phone shut. "They're on their way," he said. "It won't take them long. A fire engine is already heading out this way. And the police are already near by because of a car accident."

Another accident? thought Thora. *What is going on around here?*

She glanced up. The meteor shower had grown brighter and more intense. Hundreds of sparkling stars streamed across the sky.

Suddenly, a blood-curdling roar ripped through the darkness. Louise yanked herself free of Thora's arms and ran, screaming, into the ditch alongside the road.

6

SHIVERING SHADOWS

"Louise! Where are you?" Thora brushed aside the tall grass as she and Bryce ran through the roadside ditch and towards the dark trees.

"Louise!" cried her father. "Come back here!"

The grass became taller as Thora travelled past the line of dark trees and into the woods. She lost sight of the others. Their voices grew muffled and distant. All she heard was the swish of the grass as it brushed against her shoulders.

Thora looked up. Silently, the Draconid meteor shower was still lighting up the evening sky.

Thora pushed through more grass. Her shoes were getting damp. "Louise!" she called.

Then, from the corner of her eye, she saw a small white figure. It dashed ahead of her and vanished behind a tree trunk.

"Bryce!" yelled Thora. "I see her. She's here in the woods."

No one answered.

Thora awkwardly moved through the dense grass and trees. She grasped at the low tree branches to pull herself through.

Within the shadow of the woods, she screamed, "Louise!"

Nothing moved over the spongy forest floor. No twigs snapped. No bushes rustled.

"Louise!" Thora called again.

Nothing.

Thora pushed her way deeper into the woods. The forest grew darker and darker. Now, the roof of branches above her blocked out the starlight. Darkness was draped thickly around her. Thora shivered. "I'm lost," she said to herself.

Then Thora heard a voice. A little girl's voice. Singing.

"Within the wood

There lies a house,

And in the house, a room,

Where someone sits and waits for me,

Hiding in the gloom."

"Louise?!" cried Thora. "Is that you?"

"Then someone soon will whisper

And pull me to my doom,

Within the wood,

Within the house,

Within that little room."

Thora walked nervously towards the voice. She stopped when she saw a large, rounded shape. The shape was as black as ink against the dark trees beyond. It looked far too large to be a little girl.

Is that you, Louise? Thora thought nervously.

"Yes," came a voice from the shadow. "It's me, Thora. I'm hiding in this bush."

How did she know what I'm thinking? "But I can't see you," said Thora.

"I'm right here," came the voice. "Come closer."

The black shape shivered, as if a breeze had brushed it. But there was no wind.

"Thora!" someone yelled from behind.

As Thora turned, she saw Pablo, standing with another boy from school, Zak Fisher. He held a torch, and there was blood on his face.

"What are *you* doing here, Pablo?!" Thora asked.

Pablo blinked. "We're looking for –"

A roar shook the forest. Thora turned back. The black shape shivered. It jerked and twisted, unfolding itself. Branches became knees and elbows, twigs turned into hands. Long spindly fingers reached, claw-like, towards the sky.

Thora screamed as Zak's torch partially illuminated the growing mass. Two lizard-like eyes, black and oily, blinked back at them. The shadow rose higher. It stood tall and thick and jagged as a tree. A giant hand reached towards Thora.

"Get back!" shouted Zak. He aimed his torch's beam directly at the creature's eyes. It roared again and covered its face, seemingly writhing in pain.

Suddenly, bright light grew in the woods, as though a door had been opened in a dark room. Whiteness blazed around them. Thora could see every single leaf on the ground beneath her feet.

"Get back!" Zak shouted at the creature. "Get back, you – you whatever!" He shoved the torch closer towards the oily pupils.

Thora looked up, shielding her eyes against the growing brightness. She ignored the monster's roars and stared. A second unbelievable figure was rising in the clearing.

It was a centaur.

7

~THE HOUSE IN THE WOODS

Years ago, Pablo had read a thick book about Greek myths. He remembered a half-man, half-horse creature called the centaur that was strong and fearsome. In the forest before him, the centaur was more powerful than he could have ever imagined.

The creature's long white hair fell on to his broad shoulders. His four legs ended in gleaming white hooves. The centaur's muscular arms aimed a gigantic bow at the shadowy monster. In one quick movement, his huge hand pulled back an arrow and released it into the night.

The tip of the arrow blazed with the brightness of a shooting star as it dug itself into the monster's chest.

A scream thundered against their ears as the monster ripped the arrow out and threw it down. As the blazing light fell at Pablo's feet, he saw that it was not an arrow. At least not anymore. It was a safety flare, with one end sputtering like a welder's torch. When Pablo looked up, the centaur was gone.

"Over here!" shouted a strange voice. A man was standing behind them, waving his arms at them. "Hurry!" he yelled. "Before its eyes adjust to the light!" He turned and broke into a sprint in the other direction.

Thora, Pablo, and Zak immediately ran after the mysterious man. Soon, they emerged on to the road once again.

They came to a stop by a car with its headlights off and its engine running. All of them were out of breath and panting – except for Thora, Pablo noticed. "You don't even look tired!" he said.

Thora smiled at him. "Looks like all that running at track practice finally paid off," she said.

"There's no time for chit-chat!" urged the man, swinging open the door to his car. "Quick – get in!"

Pablo held his friends back. "Wait," he said, narrowing his eyes. "How do we know we can trust you?"

"You mean, aside from the fact that I just saved your lives?" the man answered with a smirk.

Pablo hesitated.

Although Pablo didn't know the man, he didn't see any other options. "Fine," Pablo said.

As soon as all of them had clambered into the car, it shot forward. Thora, Pablo, and Zak were hurled back against their seats. Branches scraped at the car's sides.

"Turn on your headlights!" yelled Zak.

"I don't want the others to see us," the man said calmly.

"What others?" asked Thora. She turned and glanced over at Pablo, who was staring out of the back window.

"The one back there, once it recovers, can easily find us even without seeing us," said the strange man. "And there's a group of them out tonight. A scouting party. I don't want to attract their attention."

"There are more of them?" asked Zak.

"Yes," the man said gravely. "Many, many more."

The car plunged over a deep rut.

"What exactly was that thing?" asked Thora.

"It has many names," said the man. "In its own language, it calls itself *ghool*, or *gathool*. But most experts simply call them trolls."

Trolls? A lump settled in Pablo's throat.

Zak laughed. "You've got to be kidding! You mean, like in *Lord of the Rings*? That's fairy tales."

The strange man gave a bitter laugh. "Was it a fairy tale that crashed into your parents car this evening?" he asked.

Zak's face paled. "How do you know about that?"

"Hold tight!" said the man. The vehicle bounced over a series of bumps and then stopped suddenly. "I've got to get that driveway fixed," he said, opening the door. "Well, we're here. Quick, into the house."

"What about Louise?" said Thora, her voice beginning to shake. "And I have to find my brother!"

"We will," said the man. "But we won't do them any good if we let that troll catch us. Now hurry."

A dark building rose among the trees. In a single window, dim lights glowed. The place reminded Pablo of something. An old nursery rhyme from his childhood, about a house in the woods . . .

"You're all in danger," the man warned. "You can't stay out here in the car. Please. You can trust me."

Pablo looked hard at the man's face. He seemed younger than Pablo had first thought. The man had wild hair and high cheekbones. His eyes were hard to see inside the dim car. But then Pablo saw something flash in them. *Starlight.*

"Come on," Pablo said to the other two. Then he whispered to Thora, "I think he's okay." He gave her a small smile. Thora nodded back.

They slipped out of the car and followed their guide through a garden full of weeds, then on to a solid stone porch. Zak kept glancing back over his shoulder, peering warily into the darkness around them.

8

DOCTOR HOO

Pablo shivered. The night was nearly silent. In the sky above, stars still twinkled, but the meteor shower had stopped.

The mysterious man who led them into the building wore a long cape over his shirt and jeans. In the light that poured from a round window in the door, Pablo thought he saw something. In the shadows of the man's cape, he swore he saw a third arm.

Once they were inside, the man led them up a long flight of winding stone stairs, using only a torch as a guide.

"Isn't it safer downstairs?" asked Zak.

"If those creatures get inside, it won't matter where we are," said the man.

After a few minutes of climbing, Pablo was getting out of breath. "How high do these stairs go?" he asked, gasping. "We must have climbed three storeys."

"Four," said the man. "Oh, and here we are." The stairs ended. He pushed open an old, heavy oak door and ushered them inside.

"Wow!" whispered Pablo.

The eight-sided room was spacious. Tall windows on four sides faced the points of the compass drawn on the floor. Starlight flooded into the room, revealing tables and scientific equipment. The other four walls were lined with floor-to-ceiling bookcases.

The entire countryside was visible from this height. Pablo could see the edge of the quarry, and the fields beyond the forest.

Weird, thought Pablo. *I don't remember seeing a tower outside.*

"Ah," said the man. "A full moon." He walked to a window and picked up a pair of binoculars from the windowsill.

Pablo noticed how thick the stone windowsills were. *The whole place must be built from quarry stones,* he thought.

Thora grabbed his shoulder. "This room," she whispered. "It doesn't make sense. It's bigger than his whole house!"

"I know," Pablo whispered back. "What's going on?"

"Hey" said Zak. "You seem to know a lot about us."

Zak walked towards the man and stood face to face with him. ". . . But we don't even know who you are," Zak finished.

"And what were you doing back there in the forest?" asked Pablo.

The man lowered the binoculars and turned to them. "I was there because I knew that's where the trolls would meet to join forces," he said. "According to my research, it's halfway between the two entry points to the surface."

"The quarry?" said Thora. "So that weird smell was coming from those monsters?"

"Yes – to both questions," said the man.

"But who are you?" asked Zak.

"Hoo," the man said.

"Yeah, man – who are you!" said Zak.

"Um, that's me," said the man. "Hoo. *Doctor* Hoo, actually."

Pablo eyed Dr Hoo up and down, noticing the strange clothes he wore. "What kind of doctor are you?" Pablo asked.

"I'm a doctor of several things," said the doctor. "But most recently, cryptozoology."

"What's that?" asked Zak.

Dr Hoo sat down on a window seat, facing his curious guests. "It's the study of hidden or secret creatures," he answered. "The kinds of creatures whose existence hasn't been scientifically proven."

"Like Bigfoot?" asked Thora.

"Or the Loch Ness monster," added Pablo.

"Or trolls," added Zak, with a grin.

"Or the yeti, the chupacabra, unicorns, the orange pendek, or the giant squid – which, by the way, has been proven to exist," the doctor added.

"And centaurs?" said Pablo, staring at the doctor.

"Exactly. Like centaurs," Dr Hoo said. He stood up quickly, his cape wrapped carefully around him, and pointed out of the window. "Did you know that the centaur is the only creature to have two constellations named after it?"

Zak crossed his arms. "So, what's the deal with those other creatures?" he asked. "The trolls."

"And how do you know so much about them?" asked Thora.

The doctor raced over to a wooden table.

The table was covered with books, papers, and maps. Dr Hoo pointed at a pile of books at one end. "These books were recently brought to me by a colleague," he said. "She and I met online while we were both studying the *gathool*. Her great-uncle, in fact, was the first person to discover their existence. And these are his books."

Pablo walked closer and read some of the weird titles. *The Pit of Trolls. The Call of Cthulhu. Servants of the Graveyard.*

"I have been hunting through these tomes to find the creatures' weaknesses," said the doctor. "I mean, everyone knows that trolls can be destroyed by fire or acid in stories and video games. But that's not real life."

The house trembled. Books spilled off the table. In the distance, there was a roar.

"Well, I really hope you found it, Doc," said Zak.

The room shook again. This time, books fell from several of the tall bookcases. Suddenly, Zak screamed.

The doctor swung his torch around towards Zak. An insect-like creature the size of a large cat had its thick claws wrapped around Zak's head. "Get it off me!" he yelled. "Get it off!"

"Relax," said the doctor. "It's only a coconut crab. It's stuffed."

Zak threw the lifeless hulk to the floor. "Why was it hanging from the ceiling?" he shouted.

"That's the only place I had room for it," said the doctor.

A louder roar came from outside.

"It's getting closer!" said Thora.

The doctor dug through the clutter on the table. He handed each of them a small, orange pistol.

"Flare guns," he explained. "In case of emergency. Aim directly at the creature's eyes and pull the trigger. It will blind them long enough for you to run away." Then he handed out small red cartridges. "These are the flares. Keep them on you."

Pablo stuffed a couple of flares in his pockets. He held one of the flares up in front of his face. "Could one of these start a forest fire?" he asked.

"Who cares? It's better than getting caught by one of those things," said Zak. "Hey, maybe a fire isn't such a bad idea! Doc, do trolls burn?"

"The *gathool* can survive temperatures up to 1200 degrees Celsius," said the doctor. "Some of them live next to magma streams deep within the earth."

"So I guess fire's out," said Zak.

The room shook, and a spider's web of cracks appeared in several of the windows.

"Where are they?" asked Thora.

The door opened. A ghostly shape appeared at the top of the dark staircase. The doctor aimed his torch beam at it.

Standing there, blinking in the light, was a small girl in a white nightdress.

9

A BAND OF LIGHT

"Louise!" said Thora. Louise ran to her.

"I heard it again," said the little girl. "It's getting closer."

"How did you get here?" Thora asked.

"The doctor brought me," said Louise.

"Oh, she's the girl you were looking for?" Dr Hoo said. "I found her wandering outside earlier."

"Dr Hoo, did you find the creatures' weakness?" Pablo asked. "Is there a way to stop them?"

Dr Hoo picked up one of the books from the pile on the table. "Yes, I'm afraid there is," he said.

"Afraid?" repeated Thora.

"You're not going to like it," said the doctor, flipping through the pages. "At least not right now, because it can't help us. Sunlight is the one thing that can destroy the *gathool*."

"There's at least seven hours until dawn," said Zak.

Thora shook her head. She felt weird talking about this. How could any of it be true? But she had seen the monster with her own eyes. Everyone else in the room had seen it too. And she had heard it singing to her in the forest. In Louise's voice. Trying to lure her closer. To trap her.

"Listen, I know those things out there are real," said Thora. "But are you sure about sunlight? I mean, that really does sound like a fairy tale. The sun comes up and turns a troll into stone?"

"It has something to do with their chemical makeup," said the doctor. "Their bodies can't process the sun's radiation. Which is probably what drove them to live underground in the first place." He tossed the book aside and grabbed another. "And they don't exactly turn to stone," he added. "It's more like meteoric rock. It's in their DNA. Some scientists think that's how the trolls got to Earth in the first place. On rocks from outer space. Meteors, maybe."

Dr Hoo furiously flipped through the pages of the book.

"Folklore usually does contain at least a small element of truth," he pointed out. "Ah, here it is."

He read aloud. "An ancient prophecy among the *gathool* has warned them for centuries of a deadly 'band of light' that could destroy their species. But the *gathool* vocabulary is small; their mouths are limited in the sounds they can make. So few words must stand for many things. 'Band' can also mean 'ring,' 'circle,' or 'sphere.' 'Light' can also stand for 'gold,' 'shining,' or 'pain.' Most experts believe the old tradition of sunlight being harmful to trolls is true. And since the two most powerful rings of light are obviously the sun and –"

The doctor broke off. "There's something outside," he whispered.

Dr Hoo quietly walked over to a window. The others followed him.

Louise began to whimper. Thora put her arm around the little girl.

"What's over there?" asked Pablo, pointing past the field.

"That field is straight east of this house," said the doctor. "It runs parallel to County Road One."

"That's back towards the Tooker house," Pablo said. "And the accident where everything started."

"Precisely," said Doctor Hoo. "You see, according to the old survey maps of Zion Falls, there's a deep well over there. It's likely the trolls used it as an entry point to the surface, as well as the tunnels in the old quarry."

"I know that well!" said Pablo. "It's on the land next to ours. We were always told to stay away from it."

"Why did they need an entry point?" asked Zak. "I mean, what do they want? Why are they here?"

"They want to take back the surface world," said the doctor. "Thousands of years ago, their kind dominated humans. They raised us like livestock."

"Like cows?" asked Pablo.

"More like hamburgers," Dr Hoo said, smirking. "Those creatures out there are hungry. They have travelled from far underground and they need food. *Us.*"

"Something's moving out there!" said Thora. She pointed towards the line of trees at the edge of the field.

Tall shadows swayed beneath the motionless branches.

Pablo looked out at the field and the trees and the sky. He saw something that reminded him of science class. They had been studying astronomy, which is one reason he and Thora and Bryce were watching the meteor shower that night. Their teacher had been talking about the planet Earth and how it was a part of a larger solar system. Solar. The ring of light.

"That's it – the moon!" Pablo blurted out. "That's how we can defeat the trolls. Not in seven hours, but right now!"

Everyone stared confusedly at Pablo. Just as Pablo was about to explain, the house shook more fiercely than before. Windows broke. Shelves toppled. Something made a loud crash at the bottom of the staircase.

"I have to slow them down," said the doctor, moving from the window.

"Where are you going?" asked Zak.

As the doctor stopped at the door, he swirled his cape around him like a robe. Once more, Pablo was sure he saw a third arm held closely to the doctor's side. "Do not open this door," Dr Hoo commanded.

"But, Doctor, I figured it out," said Pablo. "We can use the moon to –"

"I repeat, stay right here," said Dr Hoo. "And do not open this door under any circumstances!" He gave Pablo a quick, knowing look, and then shut the door behind him. They heard a sharp metallic click as the door sealed shut.

"Did he just lock us in?" said Zak. "I think he just locked us in."

A steady bluish-white light poured out from the keyhole and the space beneath the door. It blazed brighter and brighter, as if a searchlight were on the other side.

Another crashing sound rose up from below. Louise started to cry. Thora grabbed her and ran to the centre of the room.

"Thora," said Pablo, "remember what Mr Thomas was talking about in science class last month?"

Thora was busily checking her flare gun to see if it was loaded. "What?" she said.

"The moon!" Pablo repeated. "It doesn't produce its own light. The moon only glows because of –"

"Reflected sunlight!" Thora exclaimed, remembering. "Do you think it will work?"

"If the fairy tales are real," Pablo said.

10

A KNOCK AT THE DOOR

"First, we have to get them away from the trees," said Pablo.

"What are you two talking about?" asked Zak.

The octagonal room stopped shaking. The crashing sounds from below also stopped.

"The moon," said Thora. "The full moon is coming up."

"Yeah, so?" said Zak.

"So, that's sunlight," said Pablo.

"Sunlight kills trolls. Or turns them into meteoric rock," Thora said. "Whichever."

Zak stared at the full, yellow disc rising above the tops of the distant trees. "That's brilliant!" he said. "Better than anything the doc came up with, anyway."

That's not true, Thora thought. *Dr Hoo did mention there was a full moon. But –*

Thora's thoughts were interrupted by a knock at the door. Everyone froze.

"Let me in," said a familiar voice.

"Dr Hoo, is that you?" asked Pablo.

"Of course it is," came the reply. "Don't worry, the trolls are gone. I was able to scare them off."

"Finally, some good news," said Zak. He stepped towards the door.

"No!" Thora yelled at Zak. Then she lowered her voice to a whisper. "It's a trick."

"Thora, just let me in," repeated the voice. "Now."

"But you told us not to open it," she answered.

They heard the doctor chuckle. "So I did," he said. "But it's all over now. The creatures have moved outside."

Thora shook her head at the others. "The real doctor would use his key," she whispered. She remembered the troll back in the forest clearing and how it had sung to her – it had spoken using Louise's voice.

"Did you find Louise out there?" Thora asked.

"But she's right –" Zak began.

Thora grabbed his arm and squeezed it. She also turned to look at Louise and put her finger to her lips.

"Did you, Doctor?" Thora repeated. "Did you find Louise?"

There was a pause.

Then the doctor chuckled softly. "Yes, Thora, I did," he said. "She's standing right here with me."

"Let me in," came a little girl's voice. "I'm scared."

Louise began to shake. She clutched Thora's leg with both her arms.

"I don't like it out here," came the false voice again. "Please let me inside, Thora. Please, open the door."

Zak aimed his flare gun at the door.

"Now what do we do?" he whispered.

"It's coming," said the voice, this time more loudly. "Thora, it's coming closer. Don't let it get us! Let me in!"

The real Louise pulled away from Thora. She ran to the door and pounded on it. "Get away from us, you monster!" she screamed.

A tremendous roar rattled the door on its frame. Then a deep, angry voice roared out. "You will be my dinner, you little brats!"

11

~DESCENT FROM THE LIBRARY

Louise screamed and ran back to Thora.

Zak walked over to a broken window and looked down. "So we need to get those monsters out in the field under the moon?" he asked. "If I can get down from up here, I could run out there and make them follow me."

"We'll need some rope," agreed Pablo.

Thora, Zak, and Pablo raced through the room, searching through shelves and drawers and piles of cardboard boxes.

All of them were rifling through the room, desperate to find something useful.

"Up there!" Louise cried out. Everyone looked up to where she was pointing. Coils and coils of rope hung from hooks, attached to the ceiling.

The boys yanked down all of the rope and tied two lengths of it together. Then they threw the free ends out of the east and the south windows. Pablo and Zak climbed up on the sills, ready to abseil down the smooth rock walls.

"I can run too, you know," said Thora.

"Someone has to watch the kid," said Zak, pointing at Louise. He looked out of the window, but just as he was starting to lean out, he collapsed to the floor. Pablo and Thora ran to him.

"I . . . I can't stand," Zak said. Pablo and Thora pulled him into a chair.

"It must be the shock," said Pablo. "It's finally caught up with you."

"What do you mean?" asked Thora.

"Zack was in a car accident earlier this evening," Pablo explained. "And his parents vanished."

"Are you going to be all right, Zak?" Thora said worriedly.

Zak bent over, his face in his hands. "This can't be happening to me," the boy muttered.

"Zak can't make the sprint to the field," Pablo explained.

Thora bent down and whispered to Louise, "You have to look after him for us, okay?"

The little girl nodded. "I want a flare gun," she whispered back. Thora smiled.

Zak groaned into his hands. "Watch him," Thora repeated to Louise.

She and Pablo returned to the windows, gripped the ropes, and swung their legs over.

"Be careful," Louise whispered.

"You too," said Pablo.

They began to descend. Below them, the house's windows blazed with bluish-white light.

Quickly, the two climbers shimmied down the ropes. Doctor Hoo had said the library room was five stories above the ground. It felt much higher to Pablo. The outside walls of the octagonal tower were made of smooth stone blocks.

Because their windows faced different directions, Pablo and Thora couldn't always see one another as they descended to the ground. But Pablo heard Thora grunting and breathing hard like he was.

Then, just as Pablo was lowering himself past a window, the light from within went out. The window's glass was gone, and curtains fluttered towards him.

A heavy hand as large as a tree trunk reached out through the window. Its seven fingers opened and shut like a metal trap.

Pablo pushed himself away from the smooth wall. He swung away from the hand, his body spinning on the rope. As he neared a window on the other side, its glass shattered. Another hand, as large as the first, twisted outward, hunting for prey.

Pablo's momentum propelled him directly towards the hand. He loosened his grip on the rope so he'd slide down faster. Ten feet beneath the grasping claws, he tightened his grasp. The rope burned like fire as he came to a stop.

Pablo looked up at the angry hand above him as it clawed through the air. It pulled itself back inside the window. Then, just as Thora dropped down, the hand shot out again. Its rough fingers grabbed her legs.

"Pablo!" Thora yelled. "Help!"

Pablo tried to climb back up, but his palms were bloody from their slide down the rope. It felt as if a knife had sliced into his hands.

"Move, Thora!" he shouted.

Thora kicked at the huge hand as it pulled her towards the window. A creature hissed from inside the house. Then, a deep blackness yawned open from within the window. The troll was opening its mouth!

Pablo suddenly remembered his flare gun. He tugged it from his belt. But just as he was about to fire, he heard a fizzing sound above him.

A flare hit the troll's hand and exploded. Its blaze lit up the darkness like a tiny white sun. The stinking breath of the monster struck Thora's face as its scream burst through the window. The hand writhed in pain and released the girl's legs.

The two climbers looked up. A small white face was staring down at them from the library window. Louise waved at them, a flare gun in her other hand.

Then Zak's face appeared. "I tried to stop her," he shouted.

Pablo hurried down the rope. But the pain in his hands became almost unbearable, so he had to pinch his feet together to support the weight of his body. Slowly, he lowered himself inch by inch towards the ground until his bare feet hung only a few yards from the earth.

As his feet hit the grass, a huge crash shook the entire house as a troll burst through the wall and on to the ground.

12

Troll Chase

"Run!" Zak shouted from the window.

Pablo fell to the grass in a crouch. Thora landed a few feet away. They both leapt up and raced away from the doctor's tower.

Up in the library, Zak grabbed the flare pistol from Louise, reloaded it, and shot. A flare rocketed towards the troll and exploded on the ground in front of it. The sudden light stunned the creature. It covered its eyes and fell to the ground. *Thanks for the head start, Zak,* thought Thora, as she and Pablo ran for the field.

But in moments, Thora heard the monster roaring furiously behind them again. Then she heard the same noise coming from her right. *The creature's companions!* she realized. *They are all chasing us now!*

Without saying a word, Thora pointed towards the wall of trees that separated them from the field. Pablo nodded. They both swung off to their left, and the trolls followed them.

Two of the monsters were larger than the rest. Because of their size, they needed fewer strides to cover more ground. Their enormous feet thudded closer and closer to Thora and Pablo. And behind them came the third troll from the house. All of them were gaining speed, and all of them were hungry.

If Thora and Pablo didn't pick up speed, the trolls would soon overtake them.

Thora gritted her teeth and sucked in a lungful of air. She forced herself not to look back at the trolls. Instead, she concentrated on her breathing. She thought about track practice at school, and listened to the thumping of her feet against the soft forest ground. She thought of her brother Bryce, who always watched her race from the sidelines. She breathed deeper. Her lungs pulled in more and more air.

Then she noticed two especially large trees up ahead. The tall elms were directly in front of her. They stood only a few feet apart, and beyond them was the open field. Thora blocked out every sound, every sight, every thought. She didn't even remember that Pablo was running right behind her.

All she thought about was those trees. They were the finish line. Her goal.

She ran faster and faster, pushing all of her strength into her legs and her pumping arms. Her breath and the thudding of her feet joined in a single rhythm. *Watch me, Bryce*, she thought. *Watch me win.*

At the tree line, the first troll reached out a spiky arm. Thora ducked her head. She kept running as a second stony claw smashed right through a thick-trunked tree. The impact was so close that Thora felt the splinters brush against her cheeks. She pumped her legs even harder.

Then she was in the field.

"Keep running, Thora!" Pablo was the one screaming behind her, but Thora's ears heard Bryce, urging her onward.

Thora stared across the field. The moon was rising. She saw moonlight shining on a wire fence at the far end. That wire fence became her new finish line.

Her shoes thudded against the packed dirt of the field. Waist-high grass, hollow as straws, brushed against her calves. The thudding of her feet grew louder. The ground trembled with each step. It was the trolls – they were still following her. Their massive legs pounded like tree trunks smashing into the earth.

She didn't dare turn to look. A glance backwards would slow her down. Thora's track coach had always told her to keep staring straight ahead when she ran. Set a goal, run towards it. That's all she had to do. Just one thing in the world. Breathe and run. Breathe and run. A few hundred times.

That's all.

Thora heard another yell behind her. She recognized Pablo's voice this time, but she didn't understand what he was saying. She kept her focus on the wire fence shining in the moonlight.

The fence seemed to glitter. Thora took in deeper breaths. She lowered her head and happened to glance at her feet. *Why are my shoes all white?* she thought. *I know I put on dark ones this morning.*

The ground looked different, too. The field was white with light. The light was so intense, it was like she was running on snow. Then the light grew brighter. All colour and shadow drained away. Whiteness engulfed her like a blizzard.

Am I about to pass out? Thora thought.

Or my eyes are playing tricks on me.
Maybe I'm not getting enough oxygen.

Her feet thudded with each step. Her heart beat even faster. Her eyes were almost blinded by the light.

A hand brushed against her hair, trailing behind her like a dark flag. She stifled a scream, and pumped her arms harder.

She brushed sweat out of her eyes. She looked at the field below her. Every blade of grass, ever clump of dirt shimmered in the moonlight. Or reflected sunlight, as Pablo had said.

The heavy pounding behind her had stopped. But Thora didn't turn to look. She kept moving towards the wire fence.

"Thora!" Pablo yelled.

He was in trouble.

Thora had to help him. She slowed and quickly looked behind her.

She didn't see Pablo. Or the trolls, either. Three massive mounds of smouldering rock rested in the middle of the field. How had she missed them?

She bent over, resting her hands on her knees. The she heard a rough, scrambling sound. Thora looked up. Someone appeared from behind the rocky mound nearest her. It was Pablo, and he was grinning.

"You did it!" Pablo shouted, pointing at the rocks. "Look!"

"Huh?" Thora said. She stared hard at the mounds of rock. They resembled grotesque bodies. Chunks that looked like legs and arms and shoulders rested at the sides.

And all three had thick, boulder-sized heads.

She couldn't speak. She could only stare, wide-eyed, at the petrified trolls.

"You led them into the moonlight, and they turned to stone!" said Pablo. "It worked! It really worked!"

Thora fell in a heap on the ground, smiling. Her legs felt like they were on fire. Her eyes burned from her own salty sweat. Her chest heaved with each breath. But she didn't care. She was too happy to care.

13

THE HUNTERS

Pablo sat in the field next to Thora, quietly waiting for her to catch her breath after the desperate race with the trolls. He gazed up at the sky. The full moon sailed serenely overhead, oblivious to the fact that it had saved their lives. The meteor shower was over, but for some reason, the stars seemed to glow with an added brilliance.

"We just lived through a fairy tale," Pablo finally said.

Thora nodded. "But this isn't the happy ending," she said.

"No, not yet," Pablo said.

He knew they still had to find Bryce, and Zak's parents, and take Louise back to her father. They had to find out what had happened to Doctor Hoo, too.

And Pablo still had questions about the centaur he had seen back in the clearing, and about the third arm he had glimpsed beneath the doctor's cape. Not to mention the strange light that seemed to extend outwards from Thora as she ran through the field. But all that could wait. Right now, here in this moment, Pablo felt hopeful.

Something had changed that night for all of them. For him and Thora and Zak. And even for little Louise.

And somehow, Pablo knew it was just the beginning . . .

ABOUT THE AUTHOR

As a boy, MICHAEL DAHL persuaded his friends to celebrate the Norse gods associated with the days of the week. (Thursday was Thor's Day, his favourite!) Dahl has written the popular Library of Doom series, the Dragonblood books, and the Finnegan Zwake series.

ABOUT THE ILLUSTRATOR

BEN KOVAR was born in London. He trained in film and animation and spent several years as an animator and art director before moving into writing and illustrating fiction. He lives in an attic, likes moisture, and has a fear of sunlight and small children.

Notes on the Gathool

"Below each layer of earth where the gathool dwell, there is another layer, and another species of troll."

— Orson Drood, *Guide to the Gathool*

Like Mr Drood, I've dedicated my life to studying the gathool, or trolls. I've learned more about the different troll species than any human.

GATHOOL — the gathool consider themselves to be the pure-blooded trolls. Violent and warlike, they see humans as worthy of nothing but fuel for a hungry troll's belly. They undergo centuries of hibernation between assaults on Earth's surface. When they awaken and surface, they feed and destroy until everything is consumed. Afterwards, they return to their slumber beneath the earth until resources — humans — grow to abundance once again.

DRAKHOOL — smaller and more peaceful than other gathool, these trolls are every bit as strong and quick. They wish to live in peace with humankind, rather than destroy them. They have horns and tusks, and look similar to the minotaur of Ancient Greek myth.

AGNA GATHOOL — the descendents of true dragons, the agna gathool, or fire trolls, resemble dinosaurs. They have red-hot tongues, and are capable of spraying fire from their jaws.

The Gathool Vocabulary

The gathool language doesn't have many words, and the pronunciation is usually straightforward. However, many gathool words have several meanings, so translating the language is quite a challenge. Here are some of the words I've managed to decipher...

GATHOOL (guh-THOOL) — true trolls. The gathool use the word to describe all of troll-kind, but reserve another word for drakhool, their peaceful brethren.

DRAKHOOL (druh-KOOL) — trolls of the earth. The gathool see the drakhool as their soft-hearted, inferior siblings.

HOOLOO (hoo-LOO) — one with two souls. An individual who is born from one troll parent and one human parent. Also referred to as a half-blood.

PRAK TARA (PROK TAR-uh) — the bearers of light. The phrase refers to the children of the stars, or the star-touched ones, who are fated to oppose the trolls in a grand battle for control of Earth.

THYUL HU (THEE-uhl HOO) — ones who cannot be trusted. The phrase can refer to snakes, servants, or treacherous individuals.

Benjamin K. Hoo

FROM TROLL HUNTERS: BOOK 2

DARK TOWER RISING

Bryce Gamble couldn't remember where he was. Hard ground pressed against his back. His body was cold, yet pale sunlight felt hot on his face. So hot that it hurt. A breeze ran over his body as strange, dark fingers seemingly reached towards him. Bryce tried to focus. The fingers slowly turned into tree branches waving high above him. Where was he? All he could remember was a battle in the darkness. Huge arms, glowing eyes, bristling fangs. Something was being hunted.

Yes. He had been hunting for someone last night. A little girl. But not just her. He was hunting for humans. Any humans.

He remembered being hungry for them.

THE BATTLE WAS WON,

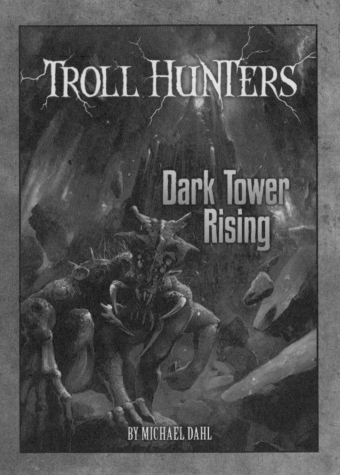

TROLL HUNTERS

Dark Tower Rising

BY MICHAEL DAHL

BUT THE WAR HAS JUST BEGUN...